Magic Toyshop

Special thanks to Val Wilding

First published in 2010 in *The Hoozles* series
First published in this edition in 2013
by Faber and Faber Ltd
Bloomsbury House
74–77 Great Russell Street
London WC1B 3DA

Printed and bound by CPI Group (UK) Ltd, Croydon, CR0 4YY
Series created by Working Partners Limited, London W6 0QT
Designed by Mandy Norman

A CIP record for this book
is available from the British Library

978–0–571–29457–2

FSC
www.fsc.org
MIX
Paper from
responsible sources
FSC® C101712

Magic Toyshop

The Naughty Croc

By Jessie Little

Illustrated by Penny Dann

faber and faber

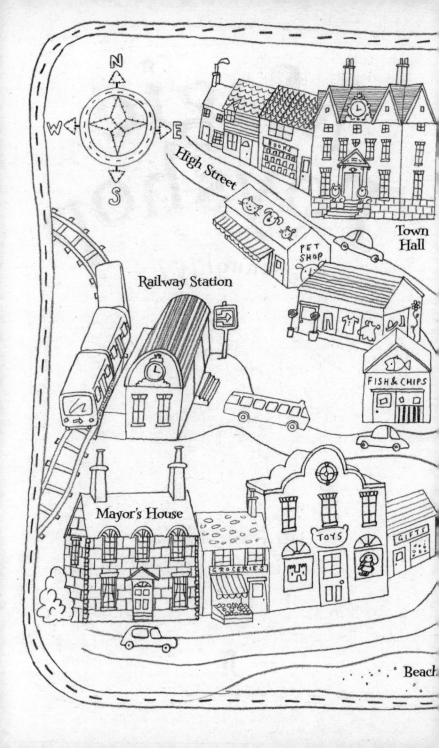

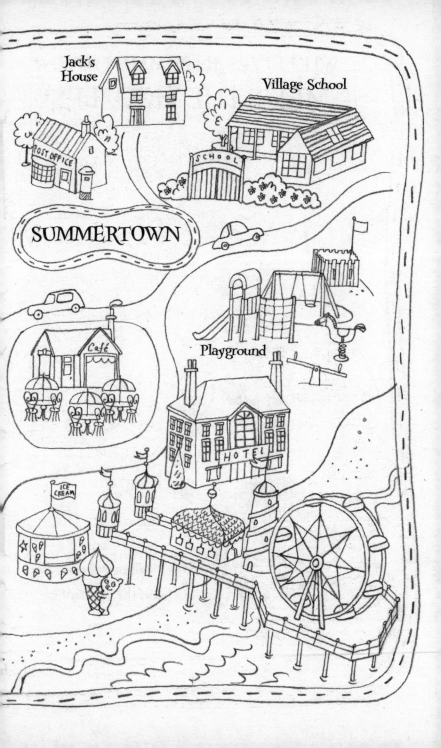

WHO LIVES IN SUMMERTOWN?
MEET THE HOOZLES!

This is
Willow and Toby

Here are Freddie
and Wobbly

Auntie Suzy
owns the toyshop!

The Hoozle Council – Grouchy, Wizard and Lovely

Nasty Croc is the
only mean Hoozle

Chapter One

'This is so exciting!' Willow
murmured to Toby, her blue teddy
bear Hoozle.

Toby snuggled up to Willow. 'A
brand-new Hoozle doesn't happen
every day,' he said in a rumbly
whisper.

Last night, Willow had discovered something extraordinary: Toby and the other Hoozles weren't just soft toys. They were actually alive! They could talk to her and move around on their own. It still gave Willow a special thrill to hear Toby speak. And now someone was in the toy shop, wanting Auntie Suzy to make a new Hoozle.

Willow was thrilled that she'd get the chance to see one being created.

'We've just moved to Summertown,' the lady at the shop counter was saying to Auntie Suzy, ruffling her son's dark hair. 'Our neighbour's children have a Hoozle each, and Jack really likes them. Don't you, Jack?'

Jack nodded and Auntie Suzy asked how they were finding life in their new house. But Jack was hanging back behind his mum, so

Willow decided to say hello to him. Her little brother Freddie was playing with one of the train sets, so she took him over too.

'Hi,' she said. 'I'm Willow and this is Freddie. We're staying with Auntie Suzy for the summer while our parents are away.'

'Hi,' the boy said. 'I'm Jack.' Then he looked down at the floor as if he didn't know what else to say.

He's shy, Willow thought. 'Have you decided what sort of Hoozle you'd like?' she asked him.

Jack shook his head.

'Maybe if I show you some of the others, you'll get a few ideas,' Willow suggested. 'This is my Hoozle – he's called Toby.'

'And this is my Hoozle,' Freddie said proudly, holding up his lion-shaped toy. 'His name is Wobbly, and he's got a football as his pocket heart.'

'His what?' Jack asked.

'His pocket heart,' Willow said. She showed Jack the little pocket on Toby's front. 'All Hoozles have a pocket like this to keep something special in to show how much you love each other. I keep a heart-shaped shell in Toby's.'

Then she pointed at the shelf above them. 'There are some Hoozles up there, too. The one shaped like an owl is called Wizard, the pony Hoozle is Lovely, and the cute penguin one is Grouchy.' She smiled up at the three Hoozles, half-expecting one of them

to smile back or wave at her. All the
Hoozles were so friendly, Willow
knew – well, apart from Croc, of
course. He was a real trouble-maker,
and Willow hoped she wouldn't have
to see him again for a long time.

'They're great,' Jack said, gazing up
at the Hoozles.

'Did I hear your mum say you'd just moved here?' Willow asked. 'You must be excited to be living in Summertown. I love it!'

Jack nodded. 'We moved in last week,' he replied. 'We haven't done much exploring yet.'

'Then you must have a look at this,' Willow said, taking his arm and leading him across the shop. 'It's Summertown, in miniature.' She loved the tiny model village that her aunt's assistant, Ricky, had made one winter. It had the sea-front, with its small wooden pier edging out into the water, the shops on the high street, the village school and, of course, all the houses.

'That is so cool!' Jack marvelled, his eyes lighting up as he gazed at the little model buildings. He pointed to an old

farmhouse set just outside the village. 'That must be our house right there.' He stooped down to peer closer at it.

'Wow – it's even got our purple front door!' He grinned at Willow and pointed to the purple T-shirt he was wearing. 'That's my favourite colour,' he said.

Willow was glad that he seemed more comfortable now.

'Ooh, those wooden animals are fun,' Jack said.

'Auntie Suzy arranges them differently every week,' Willow told him. This time, Auntie Suzy had set them up so that it seemed as if the

elephants
and zebras
were putting on a show for an
audience of other animals. 'It
really looks as if the monkeys are
cheering,' Willow chuckled, pointing
at the way they had their paws in
the air.

'And this rabbit is scared,' Freddie
giggled, showing Jack how the little
creature had its paws over its eyes.

'And look at this elephant,
balancing on one leg!' Jack said with
a smile. 'I love elephants. They always

seem so smiley and jolly, don't they?'

'Maybe you should get an elephant Hoozle,' Willow suggested.

Jack's face lit up. 'That's a great idea,' he said, and rushed over to the counter, where his mum was still talking to Auntie Suzy. 'Do you think

I could have an elephant Hoozle?' he
asked.

'Of course!' Auntie Suzy said. 'I've
never made an elephant Hoozle
before and it's high time I did. I'll
start work on him immediately. He
should be ready to collect by the end

of the day; is that okay?'

'That's wonderful,' said Jack's mum.
'Thanks very much. We'll see you
later.'

'Bye, Jack,' Willow
called as they left, and
he waved and smiled at
her.

'Right, then,' Auntie
Suzy said, rolling up
her sleeves. 'Let's get Hoozling!' She
pressed a big button on her counter
which was shaped like an owl, and
Willow watched as a painted panel

on the wall slid open. Out came a shiny pink sewing machine and a red bag, which Auntie Suzy began rummaging through.

Willow stared in delight at all the different sorts of coloured fabrics in the bag, plus scissors, thread, buttons and needles . . . everything you needed to make a Hoozle! But Auntie Suzy was frowning. 'Hmm,' she said. 'I'm not sure I've got the right material for an elephant Hoozle after all.' She glanced through the front door at where

Ricky was chatting to a passer-by outside the shop. 'I just need to pop out for a short while, okay?' she said to Willow. 'I'll take Freddie with me, but you can stay here if you'd like. I won't be long, and Ricky's there if you need anything.'

'Okay,' Willow said. When Auntie Suzy had gone, she busied herself down one of the aisles, unpacking a box of teddies which had arrived. Then, all of a sudden, she heard a loud crash which made her jump.

Willow straightened up at once

and looked around the shop . . . then
gasped with horror. There, right in
the middle of the model town, was
a mean-looking orange crocodile
Hoozle, kicking over the buildings. It
was Croc!

Chapter Two

Willow gulped. Croc was bad news.
'Stop that at once!' she said, picking
up Toby and rushing over to the
model. Lovely and Grouchy were
also leaping down from the shelves,
looking anxious.

Croc sneered at Willow as she

approached. 'I'm not scared of you,' he scoffed.

Toby leapt out of Willow's arms on to the table, fur bristling. 'Why  do you keep hanging around here breaking things? Haven't you learned your lesson?' He growled. 'Go home, before we chase you off there ourselves.'

Croc leapt off the table. 'Ha!' he jeered. 'You'd never come to where

I live; it's too noisy and smelly for a goody-goody Hoozle like you.' Then, with a horrible smile, he jumped up to the Hoozle-making station and grabbed Auntie Suzy's bag. 'And since you asked, I'm here because I don't want any more Hoozles to be made,' he said. 'So I'll take this with me!' He laughed and ran out of the back door with the bag.

'Come back!' Willow cried, but he was already gone. She scooped up Toby, her heart thumping. 'We've got to get those tools back before we have to explain to Auntie what's happened.'

'We'll come with you,' Lovely whinnied, trotting over to Willow, with Grouchy waddling behind.

Willow held her backpack open so that Lovely and Grouchy could jump in. 'I'll guard the shop,' Wizard called from up on the shelf. 'Good luck — and be careful!'

Willow put on her backpack
and scribbled Ricky a quick note:
Back soon. Then she dashed out of
the back door, the way Croc had
run. There was a trail of white fluff
leading through the small garden,

and Willow quickly realised it was the stuffing Auntie Suzy put inside the Hoozles to make them so squishy and cuddly. It must have fallen from the bag as Croc ran. 'At least we know he went this way,' she said, gathering it up as she went.

The trail led through the garden and along the alley which ran behind the row of shops. Then, as the alley led into the main street, the trail stopped. Willow looked up and down the road, but there was no more Hoozle fluff – and no sign of Croc.

She sat down on a bench with her backpack on her lap so that she could talk to her Hoozle friends. 'What now?' she hissed. 'We've got to find Croc, otherwise Auntie Suzy won't be able to make a Hoozle for Jack – or for anybody else!'

'Croc said he lives somewhere noisy and smelly,' Toby put in thoughtfully.

Grouchy flapped his wings, looking excited. 'What about the rubbish dump?' he suggested. 'That's certainly noisy and smelly.'

'Good idea! I've seen that on the town model,' Willow realised. 'Let me think . . . Just along the sea-front and left, is that right?'

Grouchy nodded. 'Shouldn't take long to get there. Let's give it a try.'

Willow set off and, after just a few minutes' walking, she found herself at the entrance to the rubbish dump. There were lots of different areas in it – a huge section for broken fridges and freezers, a place for old electrical items, and sections for wood, metal, compost, furniture . . . all sorts of things. 'Where would Croc be?' Willow wondered, wandering past an area labelled 'General Rubbish'.

'I can see toys!' said Toby in a low voice just then, and Willow stopped to look. She could see mouldy pillows, bits of an old kitchen unit, a rug with holes in . . . and yes, toys. A doll with no arms, old board games and jigsaws which had torn boxes.

But there were other toys there that didn't seem broken. A teddy who looked perfectly nice was smiling out from the pile. A stuffed dog was there too, paws dirty but otherwise fine. It made Willow feel sad.

'Why would someone throw away a toy if it wasn't completely broken?' she wondered.

Grouchy gave a shrug. 'That's just how life goes, I guess,' he said. 'Not all toys get to be loved.' He kicked the ground a little. 'I never had an owner,' he said sadly. 'I was made for a new

baby, but then the family moved
away before the baby was born.'

Lovely snuggled
against him. 'You've
got Wizard and me,'
she reminded him.
'We're glad you got
to stay with us.'

Willow cuddled
Toby close. Poor Grouchy! She was
so lucky to have Toby. 'I'm sure
you'll find someone to love one day,'
Willow told the little penguin.

But Grouchy already seemed to

have perked up. He was pointing a wing-tip at the ground. 'Hey, look,' he said. 'There are footprints there in the mud!'

The others all peered down to see. Sure enough, there were three-toed footprints leading away into the dump.

'Croc's footprints!' Willow cried.

Chapter Three

Willow followed the strange
footprints through to the furniture
area of the dump. There was a shabby,
upside-down sofa there which made
a sort of cave, and the footprints led
right inside it. Willow peered in, her
heart thumping . . . then blinked.

Staring back at her, and looking rather worried, was a black and white bird sitting on a nest.

'They were bird footprints!' Grouchy said, then hung his head. 'I should have known that.'

The bird hopped off the nest and flew away. As it did so, it knocked over a small metal box, and a stream of buttons spilled out on to the ground.

Lovely wriggled in Willow's backpack. 'Ooh, a box of eyes!' she said excitedly, seeing the buttons.

Willow smiled. To a Hoozle, she supposed buttons were eyes!

'Those shiny blue ones are nice,' Toby said, pointing a furry paw at them. 'They would be perfect on a Hoozle, wouldn't they? Maybe Jack's elephant Hoozle could have them.'

'Oh yes,' Grouchy said, nodding.
'Just right.'

Toby jumped out of Willow's
arms and gathered up the two blue
buttons, passing them to Willow.

'Good thinking,' Willow said,
putting them in her pocket. She
gazed around at the rest of the dump.
'I don't think there is anywhere else
for Croc to hide here,' she added. She
turned and headed for the way out.
'Can you think of anywhere else
that's noisy and smelly?'

The Hoozles thought for a

moment and then, just as they were
leaving the dump, an animal rescue
van drove past.

Lovely clapped her hooves together.
'The animal rescue shelter is noisy
and smelly,' she said. 'And it's just
around the corner.'

'Yes!' Willow cheered. 'Let's try that.'

They set off up the road. The sun was shining and lots of people were out and about doing their shopping or enjoying the warm weather. 'Hello, Willow,' called Mrs Morris, who was wiping tables outside her café. 'Your Auntie Suzy said you'd be visiting Summertown. It's lovely to see you! Would you like an ice cream?'

Willow smiled. 'Thank you, but I'll have to come back later,' she replied.

'Take a left here,' Grouchy

instructed from the backpack, as Willow came to a crossroads. 'Yes, there it is, just past the post office.'

The animal rescue shelter was full of cages and very noisy! Dogs barked, cats meowed, and guinea pigs gave high-pitched squeaks. 'It's definitely smelly in here, too,' Grouchy whispered, waving a wing in front of his beak. 'Ugh!'

'Hi there,' a friendly lady with curly hair said to Willow as she went in. 'Looking for a pet? You need to have an adult with you before you can take one home, you know.'

'That's okay,' Willow said politely. 'I'm just looking.'

She went into the room which housed the dogs first. A black Labrador puppy was bouncing about after a ball in one cage – he was so cute!

'Awww, look at him,' Lovely cooed. 'You know, Willow, back when your mum was growing up, she had a puppy. He was always charging around with me in his mouth. Very gentle though, he never bit me.' She glanced around to make sure nobody could see, then hopped out of Willow's backpack and waved at the puppy.

The puppy immediately came over and licked her through the bars, and Lovely burst into giggles. 'Oooh! That's so ticklish!' she cried.

Willow picked her up. 'Come on, we need to look for Croc,' she reminded the pony. 'Where might he have made a home in this place?'

They looked all around the room full of dogs but saw no place for a Hoozle home. The next room was full of cats and kittens in cages. Some were curled up asleep on fleecy blankets, others were eating or in their outdoor areas. Again, there wasn't really anywhere that a Hoozle could make a home – no dark corners or empty spaces.

'Croc must be somewhere else,' Toby said.

Willow thought Toby was probably right and turned to go. But just then, she caught a glimpse of a fluffy orange tail as it disappeared around the corner. 'Hey!' she hissed, pointing at the doorway. 'Did you see that?'

She ran after the creature and was just in time to see a flash of orange as it went into the office. It had to be Croc – they'd found him at last!

Chapter Four

Willow felt her skin prickle with
excitement as she tiptoed up to the
office and peeped inside. But there,
looking lost, was a ginger kitten.

'Meow!' it said as it saw Willow.

'You're not Croc,' Willow said,
picking it up. 'But you're way cuter

than that mean old crocodile. Aren't you, puss?'

The kitten rumbled with purrs and butted its head against Toby, who was also in Willow's arms. Its tiny paws dug into Toby's tummy, making him giggle. 'That feels funny,' he chuckled.

'Come on, you,' Willow said to the kitten. 'I don't think you're meant to be in here.'

She took the purring kitten down to the front desk and the curly-haired woman let out a cry when she saw him. 'Not again!' she said, laughing. 'How do you do it, Houdini?' She gently took the kitten from Willow. 'Honestly, he manages to get out of his cage every single day, this one. Thank you for finding him!'

Another member of staff came up to the desk just then with a purple and lilac tartan animal blanket. 'I'm going to get rid of this,' she told the curly-haired lady. 'It's been torn by the puppies, so—'

Willow couldn't stop herself interrupting. Purple was Jack's favourite colour – the fabric would be perfect for his Hoozle! 'Excuse

me,' she said quickly. 'But could I buy that blanket from you?'

The curly-haired lady smiled. 'You can have it,' she said. 'Call it a thank-you for finding Houdini.'

Willow beamed as the blanket was put in a bag for her. 'Thank you very much,' she said.

As the woman took Houdini back to his cage, Willow decided to leave the animal shelter. 'I don't think Croc lives there,' she said as she went outside. 'But we've got to find him, and soon!'

A seagull shrieked overhead, and Grouchy glared at the bird. 'Seagulls

are the most annoying birds ever,' he
muttered. 'They wake me up every
morning with all that squawking –
drives me mad!'

Willow grinned as a thought
popped into her head. 'You're a
genius, Grouchy,' she told him, giving
him a hug which made Grouchy
squirm. 'Seagulls are noisy . . . and
you get lots of them down at the pier.
Maybe Croc lives there?'

'Let's try,' Lovely said. 'And quick. Auntie Suzy will be back at the shop soon, I should think.'

The beach was crowded with holidaymakers in deckchairs, and excited squeals came from the sea as children splashed around, jumping over the waves and riding in brightly coloured dinghies. Willow and the Hoozles made their way along the old wooden boards of the pier, searching for a possible

Hoozle home. There was a little tea shop at the far end of the pier, and an amusement arcade, which was certainly very noisy, but there was still no sign of Croc.

It was only as they were walking back that Willow realised she could see through the wooden boards down to the beach below. 'Maybe we should look under the pier?' she suggested in a low voice.

'Good thinking,' Toby said, wriggling eagerly. 'It's darker and probably feels more secret down there – much more like a place Croc would want to live.'

Willow hurried down to the beach so that she could make her way underneath the pier. 'Phew!' snorted Lovely, tossing her mane. 'It's very smelly.'

The little pink pony was right. Matted clumps of seaweed clung to the iron legs of the pier and there was a sharp, salty tang in the air.

Green weed and barnacles covered the rocks nearby.

They were well away from the holidaymakers, so Willow put Lovely, Grouchy and Toby down on the ground to explore. The three Hoozles set off over the stones at once, while Willow searched too, hoping that they might have found Croc's home at last.

It was cool and quiet under the pier but after a few minutes, the silence was broken by a cry from Toby. 'Hey!'

Willow snapped her head around to check he was all right – only to see Toby tumbling backwards off a large rock. 'He's in there!' the brave bear shouted as he fell to the ground. 'In this little cave – I've seen him!'

Willow stumbled over the stones, just as Croc emerged. He had a cross look on his face, as if he didn't like being disturbed. Then, when he saw Willow, his expression changed to panic, and he turned tail.

'Don't let him get away!' Toby shouted.

Chapter Five

Willow lunged and managed to grab the little crocodile who squirmed furiously in her grasp.

Lovely cheered at the sight. 'Well done, Willow! Come on, Grouchy, let's go and look for the Hoozle-making bag,' she said, trotting into the cave.

Croc looked crosser than ever. 'You'll never find it,' he shouted, snapping his teeth together. 'I've hidden it somewhere really good.'

Willow stared at him. 'Why are you so mean all the time, Croc?' she asked as he wriggled in her arms.

Croc stuck his nose in the air. 'I like being mean,' he muttered. 'And I

never want another child to have
a Hoozle again. It would be better
for everyone if new Hoozles weren't
made at all, rather than have a child
abandon them.'

He spoke so bitterly that Willow
couldn't help but feel a pang of

sympathy. 'Is that what happened to you?' she asked.

Croc clamped his mouth shut and didn't answer.

'I won't put you down until you tell me,' Willow said.

Croc's body seemed to droop, as if he'd lost some stuffing. 'My child gave me away,' he muttered. 'To his horrible little brother who broke all his toys.'

'Well, I'm sorry to hear that,' Willow said. 'But you shouldn't go around being horrid yourself.'

Lovely and Grouchy emerged from the cave. 'We can't find the bag of Hoozle tools,' Grouchy grumbled. 'It's not in there.'

Willow's shoulders slumped in disappointment – and Croc took the opportunity to leap out of her arms and run away, disappearing among the rocks within seconds.

Willow was just about to chase after him when she heard an excited cry from Toby. 'There it is! I can see the bag!'

She looked up to see where he was pointing. Yes! There was the special bag . . . dangling out over the water from a high wooden beam under the pier. She swallowed. How were they going to get that down?

Toby seemed to read her mind. 'You stay there, Willow; it's too high for you. Us Hoozles can climb up and get it.'

Grouchy didn't look very happy about climbing up the beams. 'Oh, all right,' he muttered, following the others.

Willow watched the three Hoozles clamber up the wooden beams. Up . . . up . . . and up they went, inching nearer the bag. Grouchy quivered with discomfort. 'It's too high up here,' he moaned, shielding his eyes with a wing. 'I don't like it!' Willow held her breath while Toby pulled himself even further up the beam.

Toby grabbed the handles. 'We'll drop it down to you, Willow, all right?'

Willow nodded. 'Sure,' she called up. She kicked off her sandals and waded into the sea until she was underneath the bag. The water was lovely and cool and came midway up her calves.

'One, two, three . . . Go!' cried Lovely.

The Hoozles pushed the bag off its nail and Willow held up her arms to catch it. Yes!

'Well done, guys,' she said, sploshing out of the sea and stepping into her sandals. 'Now we have to get back to Auntie Suzy's shop. Come on!'

★ ★ ★

Auntie Suzy's toy shop was right on the sea front, so it only took Willow a few minutes to get back. Ricky waved from the storeroom at the back of the store, and Willow had just put the Hoozle-making bag on the shop counter when Suzy and Freddie came in.

'How annoying!' Auntie Suzy

said, taking off her enormous sunglasses. 'We looked for ages for the right piece of material for an elephant Hoozle, but they didn't have anything quite special enough, only this grey corduroy, which I think is a bit dull.'

Willow grinned. 'Is this any good?' she asked, holding up the purple and lilac blanket she'd got from the animal shelter. 'And I've found some lovely buttons for eyes, too.'

Auntie Suzy's face lit up. 'Perfect!' she cried, stroking the blanket. 'Oh, good work, Willow. Where did you get these?'

Willow hesitated. 'Well…' She suddenly became aware of Lovely and Grouchy, who were in her backpack, and noticed that the model of Summertown was still in a muddle.

Auntie Suzy raised an eyebrow. 'Well?' she asked. 'What's been going on?'

Chapter Six

'I…' Willow bit her lip. Was her
auntie going to be cross with her? 'I
had a bit of a Hoozle adventure,' she
confessed after a moment. 'I'm sorry
about the mess.'

'Is that so?' Auntie Suzy asked . . .
and then smiled. 'Well, I'm glad the

 the Hoozles have someone new to have adventures with.' She chuckled. 'I'm far too old now.'

Willow let her breath out in relief. 'I'll tidy this up right away,' she said, walking quickly over to the town model.

'And I'd better start work on this new Hoozle,' Auntie Suzy said, settling down in her chair.

Willow picked up all the model

buildings which Croc had knocked down and set them carefully back in place. She squinted at the model pier, wondering where Croc was now – and what he was plotting next. She didn't trust him one bit.

* * *

By the end of the afternoon, Auntie Suzy had finished the new Hoozle. He was a very jolly-looking purple elephant with a lovely grey corduroy trunk and flappy ears, which had soft silky insides. 'Now, I always like to put new Hoozles up here with the others while we wait for their new owners to pick them up,' Auntie Suzy said with a little smile. 'That way, they can get to know each other.' She reached up and put the elephant on the shelf next to Wizard. Grouchy and Lovely had also been put back there.

'There,' she said. 'Now, I'm going to make a cup of tea and see what your brother's up to, Willow,' Auntie Suzy said. 'Back in five.' She went upstairs, leaving Willow alone in the shop.

Willow immediately looked up at the Hoozles. She watched in delight as they came alive ... including the new elephant Hoozle. He stretched his trunk and shook his ears out, then

gave a slow blink and looked around.

'Hello,' Wizard said in his kindly
voice. 'And welcome. We're the
Hoozles – Wizard, Lovely and
Grouchy – and as members of the
Hoozle Council, we're all delighted

to welcome you to the world!'

'Oh!' said the elephant in a
cheerful voice. 'How very splendid
to meet you. Hello, hello and hello!
I'm . . .' He thought. 'Who am I?'

Willow let out a giggle. 'That's for
Jack to decide,' she said, smiling up at
the elephant. 'He's going to be your
new owner.'

'Oh, he is, is he?' the elephant said.
'Jolly good.' He gazed around the
shop. 'What a wonderful place this is!'

Willow cuddled Toby, thinking
what a nice creature the new Hoozle

seemed. Friendly and fun, so positive about everything – he was exactly what shy Jack needed to give him some confidence, she decided.

Just as she was thinking about Jack, the bell on the shop door jingled and in he came with his mum. 'Hi,' Willow said, pleased to see them again.

Jack smiled. 'Hi, Willow,' he said. His eyes darted around looking for Auntie Suzy. 'How's your aunt getting on with my Hoozle?' he asked.

Auntie Suzy bustled in, just as Willow was pointing up at the Hoozle shelf.

'Hello again! I heard the bell ring. Here, let me,' Suzy said, and carefully took down the elephant for Jack. 'What do you think?'

Jack's face was split with a broad grin. 'He's great!' he replied happily. 'I love the material you used – oh,

and his eyes are so sparkly.' He
flung his arms around Auntie Suzy.
'Thank you!'

Auntie Suzy looked pleased. 'You're
very welcome,' she laughed. 'Now,

did Willow explain about the pocket heart?'

Jack nodded. 'Yes, and I've got just the thing,' he said, reaching into his trouser pocket. He pulled out a little red ball. 'This is the bounciest ball I've got – it's my favourite,' he said, and popped it into the elephant's front pocket. 'And I'm going to call you . . . Bouncer,' he said to his Hoozle.

'Wonderful!' Suzy exclaimed, as Jack gave Bouncer a big cuddle.

Willow couldn't stop smiling. She felt so happy for Jack, now that he had his own Hoozle. 'They're going to have a wonderful time together,' she murmured to Toby as Jack and his mum went to pay for Bouncer. 'Just like me and you.'

Magic Toyshop

Get ready for even more

Magic Toyshop adventures!

Freddie's Hoozle Wobbly has lost his magic pocket heart! It's up to Willow to find it as they embark on their first Hoozle adventure . . .

Can Willow and the Hoozle Council
help Frank find a pocket heart and
stop Croc's mischievous plans?

Naughty Croc is trying to steal
Smooches's magical pocket heart.
Can Willow and her Hoozle friends
come to the rescue in time?

Willow can't wait for the boat trip to
Smuggler's Cove. But naughty Croc
has secretly come too! Will they find
treasure on the island?

Also in the series:

A Penguin Problem

Grouchy the penguin Hoozle
is feeling poorly, and naughty
Croc is causing trouble all over
Summertown. Can Willow and her
Hoozle pals help Grouchy get better
before Croc makes things much
worse?

The Big Parade

Everyone's excited about the
wonderful Summertown Parade. But
the town's Mayor has disappeared
so the parade might not happen. Is
Croc the naughty Hoozle behind the
trouble? And can Willow and friends
find the mayor in time for everyone
to enjoy the special day?